Oh, the THINKS you Can Think!

By Dr. Seuss

RANDOM HOUSE 🏠 NEW YORK

You can

think up

some birds.

That's what you can do.

You can think about yellow

or think about blue . . .

You can think about red.
You can think about pink.
You can think up a horse.
Oh, the THINKS you can think!

Oh, the THINKS
you can think up
if only you try!

If you try,
you can think up
a GUFF going by.

And you don't have to stop.

You can think about SCHLOPP.

Schlopp. Schlopp. Beautiful schlopp.

Beautiful schlopp

with a cherry on top.

You can think about gloves.
You can think about SNUVS.

You can think a long time
about snuvs and their gloves.

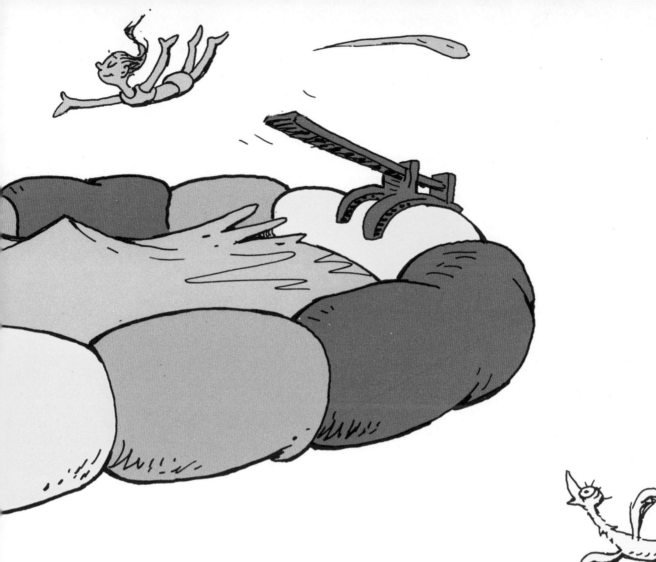

You can think about
Kitty O'Sullivan Krauss
in her big balloon swimming pool
over her house.

Think of black water.

Think up a white sky.

Think up a boat.

Think of BLOOGS blowing by.

You can think about Night,
a night in Na-Nupp.
The birds are asleep
and the three moons are up.

You can think about Day,
a day in Da-Dake.
The water is blue
and the birds are awake.

Think! Think and wonder.
Wonder and think.
How much water
can fifty-five elephants drink?

You can wonder . . .

How long
is the tail
of a ZONG?

There are so many THINKS
that a Thinker can think!

Would you dare
yank a tooth
of the

RINK-RINKER-FINK?

And
what would
you do
if
you met
a JIBBOO?

Oh, the THINKS
you can think!

Think of
Peter the Postman
who crosses the ice
once every day—
and on Saturdays, twice.

THINK! You can think
any THINK
that you wish . . .

Think
a race
on a horse
on a ball
with a fish!

Think of Light.
Think of Bright.
Think of
Stairs in the Night.

THINK!

Think a ship.

Think up a long trip.

Go visit the VIPPER,

the Vipper of Vipp.

And left!
Think of Left!

And think about BEFT.
Why is it that beft
always go to the left?

And why is it
so many things
go to the Right?
You can think about THAT
until Saturday night.

Think left and think right
and think low and think high.

Oh, the THINKS you can think up if only you try!